A Terrible Place

and Other Flashes of Darkness

D.L. Winchester

Undertaker Books

Book Cover by Joe Stout

First edition 2024

A TERRIBLE PLACE
AND OTHER FLASHES OF DARKNESS

Introduction

When I was much, much younger, my little sister's favorite movie was *The Sound of Music*. She had to watch it at least once a day, often more. Even now, almost three decades later, I can still sing most of the songs from that movie.

Of those songs, a little ditty about Maria's "Favorite Things" stands out as I sit down to introduce this collection. From geography to mortuary science, history to sports, trains to music, this collection is literally made up of a few of my favorite things.

Then I went and added a heavy dose of horror to them.

I'm not saying *A Terrible Place and Other Flashes of Darkness* is my complete response to *The Sound of Music*.

But I might be suggesting that watching that movie over and over corrupted my brain enough to make it possible.

How do you solve a problem like D.L.?

Flash fiction and horror. And lots of it.

Story Notes

GPS

I learned to read using a Rand McNally road atlas. True story. I still prefer using paper maps to navigate, and never quite learned to fully trust the GPS. Making the leap from "annoying technology" to "beast in the woods" was an easy one.

Ghost Dance

In middle school, the choir room was in the basement, next to a few old practice rooms with windows looking out onto a patch of grass and a road. I was thinking of those rooms when I wrote this, and added a cemetery for extra spookiness.

A Terrible Place

This piece on a true story that happened in the Coal Creek War. I came across the tale while researching stories of hauntings in my area (the Drummond bridge is where the original hanging occurred), and decided the best way to bring the legend into the conscious mind was to bring the story forward fifty years and add a touch of horror.

Gravedigger

The first appearance of the mortuary sciences in this collection. What's spookier than being in an old cemetery after dark? Not much. What drives away the spookiness? Money, and lots of it. What's lurking at the bottom of the grave? Horror, of course.

Good Riddance

It took a little thinking to decide on a couple of non-fatal tortures using the trocar before I put it in the victim's heart.

Midnight Train from Toyah

I wanted a train story, which naturally lent itself to a western. But how do you bring horror to a railroad? A robbery was my first thought, but incorporating horror into that was a challenge. Then I looked out into the dark landscape, saw a demon riding toward the train, and the rest was easy.

Run. Hide. Fight.

There's a couple posters that have this in large letters where I work, explaining what to do if there's an active shooter.

Grandma's Advice

I love sports, but it's damnably hard to find a new way to tell a sports story. "We won" or "we lost but learned" tend to be the main options. Then I started thinking in terms of horror, and had the idea of a stadium filled with thousands of the same face.

Consumed

A western tale that turned out to be a delightfully slow burn. At least, as slow of a burn as you can have in a thousand words.

Nostalgia

I love historic ballparks and stadiums, and hate the idea of trading modern conveniences for tradition and history. Since I'm a writer, I found a way to release some of my pent-up frustration on the subject.

Monster of the Chamber

I'm kind of surprised only one capital punishment piece made it into this collection. But if there's only one, a gas chamber tale is always a good pick. The gas chamber was a brutal execution method (technically I should say "is" a brutal execution method, since it's still on the table in some states) that lends itself well to horror.

Tattoos and Scars

I'm really not sure where this idea came from. I was thinking about a water tower, and the next thing I knew a tattoo gun was humming and the story was writing itself.

Ghost Flight

Another story born of true events. Back in the sixties, United Flight 823 crashed just north of Parrottsville, Tennessee, killing all on board. Bring it to modern day, toss in another grieving pilot, and a horror tale is born.

Counting Spoons

For this, I tried to write the scariest thing I could think of, and to me, being grabbed and imprisoned with no explanation then held for days in a boring room would be high on my list. Then being let go without answers would drive me nuts.

Beast of the Rappahannock

A piece born in the Civil War. This was a sample piece I wrote for an anthology I was thinking about publishing (and still may), but things happened, and I like it enough that I'd rather get it into the world than wait for something that may not happen.

Retort

Regular or extra crispy? Okay, I couldn't resist. But, did you know that cremation destroys your DNA? The thought of a serial killer that uses cremation to hide his victims has intrigued me for awhile, but in the interim, using a retort for a little revenge was a fun idea to pursue.

GPS

In eight hundred feet, turn right onto Landers Gap Road.

"I wish you wouldn't rely on that thing," Cody Miller said, looking down at the atlas in his lap.

"You know I'd be lost without it," his mother replied, guiding the car into the turn.

Cody rolled his eyes. They'd had this argument before, technology versus analog, and no matter how hard Cody argued for maps, his mother insisted on using the GPS.

"This road isn't even in my atlas," he protested.

"Then it'll be an adventure!"

"Maybe." He closed the atlas and stared out the window.

Ahead of them, the sun was setting over the forest. Cody's dad was waiting for them across the mountains, at their new house in Tennessee. Cody and his mom had stayed in North Carolina to finish his last week of seventh grade, and now they were heading to their new home.

"This doesn't look safe," Cody said, studying the cracked asphalt ahead of them and the steep drop to a rocky river on the right.

His mother smacked her hand on the steering wheel. "Damn it, Cody, you haven't done anything but complain since we told you about this move!"

"I didn't want to move!" Crossing his arms, he pulled his knees onto the seat. "Stupid Dad and his stupid new job. It's not fair!"

"Life isn't fair."

In five hundred feet, turn left onto Potter Mountain Road.

The car turned onto another road, leading away from the river.

"It should be." The woods outside were getting thicker, and the sun had almost finished setting. As the car bounced off the asphalt onto gravel, Cody wished he was home, not bouncing through the mountains.

You have arrived at your destination.

"What?" Cody's mother looked out into the small part of the world the headlights showed. It was a gravel road with thick trees on both sides. The only light came from the headlights and a handful of twinkling stars.

"Still think the GPS was a good idea?" Cody asked, not turning to look at her.

"It's just a malfunction. I'll reset it." The device powered down to a black screen. After waiting a few seconds, she turned it back on again.

You have arrived at your destination.

"Stupid thing; I haven't even put in the destination yet." She punched some buttons, then reset it again.

You have arrived at your destination.

Turning off the device, she looked at Cody.

"Do you know where we are?"

"On an adventure," he replied, sarcasm dripping from his voice.

"Funny. Real funny." She checked her phone. "No signal, of course."

Cody looked out the window, wondering how they'd gotten here. He hadn't been paying attention, thinking about the friends he was leaving behind and how miserable life in Tennessee was going to be.

The GPS flashed, then turned itself on.

You have arrived at your destination.

"Piece of junk." She turned it off again and threw it in the backseat.

"Well, you showed it."

She rolled her eyes. "I'm going to find somewhere to turn around. We'll go back the way we came." She put the car in drive, but when she stepped on the gas, the vehicle turned off.

You have arrived at your destination.

Cody reached into the backseat and picked up the GPS. Rolling down his window, he hurled it into the trees by the road. It bounced once, twice, and came to a rest, the dim glow of the screen marking its landing place.

His mother tried to start the car again. All she got was a clicking noise. "What the hell?"

"Yeah, this is an adventure all right." Cody opened his door. "I have to pee."

"Wait! Don't get out!"

"I'm just going to the edge of the road, Mom."

Cody stood with his back to the car, listening as his mother cursed, trying to get it to start. This was all her fault. If she hadn't listened to the GPS, they wouldn't be lost in the mountains.

Prepare yourself for sacrifice.

He looked down at the GPS, still glowing in the darkness. Was he imagining things?

The beast approaches. All hail the beast!

Behind him, he heard the sound of crunching metal. Turning slowly, he saw a massive, hairy fist rising from the crushed roof of their car.

His eyes moved from the fist up the arm to the beast's massive body. It was twenty feet tall and covered in dark hair. When he found the face, white teeth shone against the darkness, and the black eyes were pits of nothingness against the night sky.

"Cody! Run!" His mother's voice snapped him out of his trance. He sprinted down the gravel road. A roar followed him, and something flew over his head. It landed in front of him, rolling down the road ahead.

It was the car.

The ground started to vibrate as heavy footsteps approached from behind. He tried to go faster, but could barely see the road in front of him. A rock sticking out of the road tripped him, sending Cody tumbling down the hill. His body crashed into something with a metallic clang.

The thundering footsteps got closer, then a massive hand closed around him, lifting him into the air.

Kicking and twisting, he tried to break free, but the beast gripped him tighter. As the creature's mouth opened, he heard the GPS.

You have arrived at your destination.

Goodbye.

Ghost Dance

John looked out the window at the worn gray headstones. These practice rooms backed up to the old city cemetery, a burial ground that had been in use since before the college had been thought of, much less the new music building.

From the second story, he could see across the old cemetery to the new one on the other side of the highway. The green grass and marble stones reached the top of the distant hill, where the sun was setting in an explosion of color.

On the table in front of him, his computer sat open, along with a couple of binders. A blank score marked "Senior Composition" lay on the table, the one he was supposed to be finishing.

He didn't want to.

Once he did, it was over.

Outside of college, music was a hobby, not a career. John had been offered a teaching job, but even being around music every day, it wouldn't be the same as it was now, when he could play the viola to his heart's content and work with professors and visiting masters.

Reaching for the window, he opened it, enjoying the cool breeze.

No more feeling sorry for yourself, the voice in his head told him. *Time's ticking.*

Pushing aside the binders, he reached for his computer and opened the note-tracking software that would record what he played. The accuracy wasn't always perfect, but it was better than stopping every few seconds to write notes down. Wiping sweat from his brow, he reached over and opened the window. These rooms were always too hot or freezing.

Opening his case, he took out his viola. Although John joked he could play anything with strings, the violin's deeper cousin had always been his favorite. Sliding the horsehair of the bow through a rosin block, he made a couple adjustments before lifting the instrument to his chin.

Moving the bow across the strings, he played a couple of scales, watching the notes appear on the computer screen.

The sun was almost over the horizon now, a bare curve of orange visible over the top of Cemetery Hill.

"When the sun goes down, the spirits rise," John muttered.

What the fuck do you mean by that?

He shrugged. It was as good an inspiration as any, and after two weeks of struggling, if that idea made the music flow, he'd follow it.

Start in the depths of death.

That would be deep, the bottom of the scale. He found a melody: a dark, echoing sound that rose slowly, bringing the spirit to the surface.

John looked out the window and almost dropped the viola. Across the cemetery, a faint, transparent head rose from every headstone. They turned to him, the look on their faces clear.

Keep playing.

He did, bringing the spirits to the surface. Ghosts crowded the cemetery, transparent figures in clothing from various eras, from colonial coats and breeches to modern suits, from nightgowns to pantsuits.

Having brought them up, John switched to a lively medley, his bow moving quickly across the strings. In the cemetery, the spirits found partners and began to dance. John wondered if anyone else was seeing this, a driver on the road or a student looking out their dorm window. Surely someone else saw them; there were thousands of ghosts out there!

But no screams drifted into the practice room, no cars screeched to a halt on the highway.

John transitioned into a slow, somber tune as the dancers came together. Swaying gently, they let John lead them through a sad ballad, the notes floating across the cemetery on the breeze. As the song ended, a tall man in a top hat turned to look at John, circling a finger in the air.

Speed it up!

John thought about the Appalachian Mountains, the fiddle tunes passed down through the generations. They weren't made for the viola, but maybe...

The bow danced over the strings, and across the cemetery groups formed to dance reels, the spirits moving so quickly they looked like swirls of smoke as he increased the tempo of his own playing. With a final pull, the tune's closing notes sailed across the cemetery.

Someone tapped on the door. "Five more minutes, John!"

Five minutes. Damn. He wanted to stay all night, to spend as long as he could with the dancing spirits. "Okay," he called.

Time to play them home.

Starting with high, light notes, he slowly went deeper, watching as the spirits returned to their graves, bodies fading into the ground. As the last top hat disappeared underground, John played the last long, deep notes before setting down his bow.

He hadn't realized how hard he had been playing. Sweat soaked his t-shirt. With a sigh, he returned the viola to its case and reached for his water bottle.

It felt like a dream. Hundreds of souls called from the grave by his music, dancing in the moonlight, then returning to their eternal slumber...

His computer beeped, and he reached for it.

Would you like to save your composition?

Would it work again? Would these same notes call the dead from their graves to dance in the moonlight?

Could he travel the world, calling back the dead for a few fleeting moments of happiness? Would adoring crowds watch, gathering in cemeteries to see their loved ones return for the dance?

Part of him wanted to know.

Part of him thought once was enough.

Moving the mouse, he made his decision.

A Terrible Place

Jacob Potts walked along the railroad tracks, a rope coiled over his shoulder. Above him, a full moon illuminated the valley. Behind him, the sounds of a barn dance faded in the distance.

He'd finally done it. Finally worked up the nerve to ask Diane Whitley to dance. It had taken him almost an hour, standing in the corner watching her talking to her friends. She was beautiful; brunette hair, blue eyes, country charm. Nothing like the girls he'd known down in Knoxville.

She'd even said yes to his stuttered question, but before they made it to the dance floor, Charlie Loran had cut in, pushing Potts away and taking Diane's hand.

"Don't take pity on the City Rat," Loran had sneered.

City Rat. That's all they'd called him since he arrived in Briceville after his parents died. A distant cousin had been the only one willing to take him in, and she had her own problems, as the pile of bottles in the trash can showed. But she needed a hand around the farm, and Jacob could do chores as well as the next boy. So for three months now, he'd slopped pigs, milked cows, and felt his life collapse around him.

As Charlie and Diane had walked away, he had leapt for Charlie's back, but his henchmen grabbed him and carried him outside.

Doug and Dennis, their names were. Each of them had six inches and two hundred pounds on Jacob. Against both, he didn't have a chance.

They'd beaten him mercilessly, bouncing him between the two of them until Charlie came outside and joined them. Diane had watched, standing against the wall smoking a cigarette.

"He won't bother you again," Charlie had promised her when they were done, Jacob lying in a bloodied heap on the ground.

Diane had blown a smoke ring, curling her beautiful lips into a circle to loft the shape into the air. "Good. I honestly don't care if I ever see him again."

His ribs still hurt from the beating, but that was temporary. Soon that pain, all of the pain, would be gone.

No more Charlie and Diane.

No more Doug and Dennis.

No more being the school punching bag.

No more Cousin Mae and her drinking.

No more chores.

No more bullshit.

He reached the old railroad bridge and uncoiled the rope he'd taken from the barn. Forming a noose on one end, he lowered it through the trestle, then tied the other end to one of the beams. There were already grooves in it, he noticed, like something had been tied there before. Following a narrow footpath to the creek below, he was just in time to see the rope floating away.

"Shit!" Running after it, he waded out into the cool water to grab it. A cow on the far bank stared at him. He stared back, rope in his hands, pants soaked to the knees. The creature turned away, and Jacob splashed back to the bank. Climbing to the bridge, he tied the rope again, making sure it was secure.

I'm nervous, he thought, checking the knot a third time. *Who wouldn't be.*

Feeling the pain in his ribs flaring up, he slid down the embankment downstream of the bridge. The rope floated in the middle of the creek, and Jacob splashed out to get it.

What the hell? Standing there in the water, he looked at the rope in his hands. It was perfectly ordinary, nothing strange about it, nothing that would cause the knot to slip.

This time, he climbed up from underneath, looping the rope over the beam, then tightening the noose around his neck. Taking a deep breath to steady his nerves, he leapt from the piling.

With a splash, he plunged into the water. The creek was deeper here, enough for him to be fully submerged. Breaking the surface, he looked around. The damn cow was back, and it had a friend now, silently watching from the creek bank.

"What are you looking at?" Jacob called angrily. The two cows stared back in silence. A cool breeze drifted through, making Jacob shiver. Reaching down, he grabbed a rock from the creek bed and hurled it at the cows before pulling the noose off and gathering the rest of the rope.

Jesus. I know these knots are tight. What the hell is going wrong? Climbing back up the piling, he looped the rope over the beam again, and worked the rope into a knot. Giving the rope a firm tug, he made certain it was secure before placing the noose around his neck and falling away.

The rope caught, bringing his body to a sudden stop, but death didn't come. Jacob twisted in the air, grabbing for the rope, struggling to stop it from digging into his neck and cutting off his oxygen.

A scene flashed before his eyes. A bridge, this bridge, a group of men standing underneath looking at something. Was this the future? No, the clothes were older. This was the past, something that had already happened. The men were soldiers, staring up at a body hanging from the same beam he had tied his rope to. The body slowly rotated, spinning at the end of the taut line. As it came around again, the face lifted, and seemed to look into Jacob's soul.

"This is a terrible place to spend eternity!"

The deep voice shook the bridge, and Jacob realized he was falling again. Hitting the water sent a fresh bolt of pain through his injured body, and he struggled to make it to the shore. Crawling onto the muddy bank, he laid his head on a rock and passed out.

He woke feeling worse than when he'd fallen asleep. Not that sleep had been easy. It felt like every time he'd closed his eyes, he'd seen the man hanging from the bridge, staring at him.

Sitting up, he saw the cow watching him from across the creek.

"Go away, damn it!" he yelled, getting to his feet and throwing a rock at it.

Damn cows.

The rope lay on the muddy riverbank, the noose still tied in the end.

Jesus. I should be dead!

Climbing the embankment, he walked along the railroad tracks past the now-empty barn where the dance had taken place. A half-mile farther on, a small house lay between the railroad and highway. He headed toward it, peeling off his muddy clothes and shoes on the back porch before going inside.

Mae was sitting at the kitchen table, a steaming cup of coffee in her hand. Potts knew there was probably something else in the coffee, but didn't say anything. "Well, look what the cat dragged in," she started. "I wasn't expecting you to start your drunken carousing so soon, but I guess you've chosen your own damn schedule. Looks like you ran into plenty of trouble too."

Jacob looked down to see a network of green, purple, and blue bruises on his body.

"Don't think this shit gets you out of your damn chores either. Get some clothes on and get to work. You don't want to sleep, that's on you!"

Jacob walked to the door, then stopped. "Cousin Mae, has anything ever happened at the old railroad bridge?"

"What old railroad bridge? You gotta be more specific, boy!"

"Down past the Gentry barn, where it crosses Coal Creek."

She froze for a moment, then shook her head. "Drummond Bridge. Of course that'd be the one you'd ask about." She got to her feet and shuffled through the house. Jacob waited in the kitchen until she came back, holding a picture frame. "They hung my older brother from that bridge. He got in a drunken fight over a girl, they said he killed a soldier, and the rest of the soldiers lynched him. 'Eye for an eye,' all that bullshit. Ma and Pa wrote the army, the governor, anyone they could think of, but no one ever decided to get involved." She turned the picture frame around. "This is my brother, Dick."

Jacob froze, recognizing the face in the picture as the man he'd seen while hanging under Drummond Bridge

"You look like you've seen a ghost," his cousin said.

"I think I have..." Jacob stammered. "I think he saved my life."

Mae raised an eyebrow, then shook her head. "Fred Travis said the same thing when he tried to hang himself off the bridge. Said the damn knot wouldn't stay tied, and finally ol' Dick showed hisself and told him to cut it out."

John nodded. "That's about what happened to me."

Mae took a sip of coffee from her cup. "Reckon if my brother thinks you're worth keepin' alive, you'll be good enough to have around here. Go change out of them wet clothes. We got chores to do."

Gravedigger

The shovel pierced the dark earth, and Mark tossed the contents over the side of the hole. Reaching into his shirt pocket, he pulled out a bandana and wiped his face. He should be home, a hot shower washing away the dirt and grime of another day. But a service that afternoon had gone long, and the graves at Mount Moriah Cemetery had to be dug by hand. So he returned the bandana to his pocket and kept digging.

He was almost done when he drove the shovel into the dirt and felt something give way under it.

"Fuck." It was probably a casket, which meant he would be back at the crack of dawn to re-dig the grave after spending half the night working with the caretaker to find an unoccupied spot.

But as he pulled the blade out, he saw a flash of metal. Dropping to his knees, he brushed the dirt away, revealing rotting wood, and through the hole his shovel had made...

"Gold! Holy shit!"

Jumping to his feet, he peered out the top of the hole. No one was in the cemetery or at the old church next door. Turning, he looked at the sun. About thirty minutes to dark.

Grabbing the shovel, he went to work clearing the dirt from around the box. By the time he was done, he'd uncovered a wooden box about a foot square and six inches deep.

"Jesus!" Mark saw a future that didn't involve spending every day in the dirt, digging graves in the hot sun and cold winter. He could retire, buy some land in the mountains and build the cabin he'd always dreamed of.

It was his, after all. He'd found it, and there was no one to object to his claim, especially if he never told anyone. If he had to give an explanation, he'd say it was an inheritance.

Bending his knees, he put both hands under the box and tried to lift. It didn't move, so he pulled harder, with no result.

Who knew gold was so heavy?

Finally, he gave a strong yank, and the rotten wood gave, sending him tumbling onto his ass.

"Fuck." He looked at the box in the fading light. It'd take a crane to get it out of here, something mechanical at least, and getting it in here would be almost impossible.

Wait.

His lowering device.

He could slide a piece of plywood under the box, then use the straps of his lowering device to winch it up.

Looking to the west, he saw the top of the sun sinking under the horizon. By the time he got back, it would be completely dark.

Perfect.

An hour later, he carried the metal lowering device toward the grave, where he'd set up two portable work lights. That was a risk, but if anyone noticed, he'd just say he was working late.

Dropping into the hole, he used the shovel as a lever to help slide the plywood under the box. Once that was done, he climbed out and set the lowering device over the hole, repositioning it so both straps would be under the box.

Jumping back in the hole, he slid the first strap under the plywood and attached the loose end to the other side of the device. As he started to slide the second one underneath, the board tilted toward him, knocking him off balance.

Getting up, he shook his head. Must not have been set well. Picking up the strap, he reached toward the board again.

The plywood split as a human form burst through it. Slivers of rotting wood and gold coins pelted him as he fell back into the dirt.

White bone shone in the light as something climbed out from under where the box had been. Standing over Mark, the skeleton looked down at him, empty eye sockets seeming to see everything he'd ever wanted to hide.

The jaw opened. "Where are you going with my treasure?"

The voice froze Mark in place. It wasn't a booming roar or a soft whisper, it was almost conversational, with just a slight wheezing tone to suggest its owner wasn't a fully-formed human.

"I didn't know it belonged to anyone," Mark stammered. "I didn't know you were under there, I thought someone abandoned it."

"Abandoned it?"

Mark nodded, not trusting himself to speak.

"You were going to spend it on yourself?" The skeleton bent over, giving Mark a better view of the empty eye sockets.

"Well, yes, I do have some things it would be useful for."

"Do you think," it whispered, jaw clattering as it came together and fell away, "that I buried my gold because I wanted it spent?"

"Well, no... I'll put it back! I won't tell anyone!"

Laughter erupted from the white skull. "I know you won't tell anyone." A bony hand wrapped around Mark's neck, lifting him from the dirt. "You won't tell anyone at all."

In a burst of motion, Mark was face down in the bottom of the hole, two bony hands pressing his head into the dirt. He thrashed and twisted, trying to get away, but the hands pressed harder.

"The gold is mine," the skeleton wheezed. "Now and forever, the gold is mine!"

Mark's body finally went limp. As his soul floated away, he watched the skeleton gather all the gold and put each piece into the hole it had emerged from. With a last look at the gravedigger's body, it returned to the hole itself, bony hands scooping dirt into place until no sign of the treasure remained.

Good Riddance

He is awake now, fearful eyes desperate for details but finding only a white ceiling. I know he can't see me, standing in the corner of the room studying my work. Three rolls of duct tape wrap around the porcelain table, holding him in place. A single piece covers his mouth, keeping him from screaming.

This funeral home has been abandoned for almost ten years, the victim of a recession in a supposedly recession-proof business. I bought the place at auction from the tax office. As long as I keep the taxes paid and the lawn mowed, no one from the city cares what I do with the place.

I take that back. They probably would care about what is in store for the man on the table. So would the district attorney, the sheriff, and a jury of my peers.

But that's it.

He's squirming now, trying to loosen the tape. Approaching, I take a scalpel from the metal tray at the head of the table and hold it over his face. His eyes focus on it, the perfect instrument to cut himself free.

"Do you remember, Mr. Pickett," I whisper, and his eyes widen in recognition. "You bent me over this very table, taking a 'fee' for your mentorship. Do you remember threatening to destroy me if I ever told anyone?" The scalpel drops an inch, swinging over his nose. "Do you?"

His increase in effort tells me he remembers.

"Ten years, you've been alone. Or have you? Have there been other young men, willing or unwilling, who have kept you company since this place closed?" He shakes his head from side to side, and I laugh. "You liar." Leaning over, I move my face into view.

"I buried them. Car accidents, suicides, other tragedies, their families always telling me what a good friend you'd been to them. And yet, you never made it to their funerals. Did you know you were the reason for their deaths? Did the shame of what you'd caused keep you away?" I lay the scalpel on the table next to his head. "You were almost the death of me, but I decided I'd rather be the one to finish *you.*"

Pulling on a pair of latex gloves, I walk to the side of the table. "There are so many things I want to do to you. Part of me wants to be brutal, to slice your dick off and shove it in your mouth until you choke!"

The head shakes again, and I laugh. The fool is scared, too scared to even cry. "Don't worry. I thought about it more, and decided to use what you taught me instead."

I turn on a faucet, and a familiar gurgling sound comes from the sink at his feet. Picking up a metal instrument, I hold it over him.

"The trocar."

A hollow tube with a needle-sharp point appears in his vision, and his eyes widen.

"I bought a new one for the occasion. I can afford it; business has been good since you closed."

Touching the tip of the trocar to his stomach, I put pressure above and to the right of his belly button, a place uncovered by the tape.

"You remember teaching me to aspirate, right Mr. Pickett? You told me this probably sucked better than I did." I smile. "Let's find out."

With a firm push, the skin yields, and the metal tube slides into his belly. Yellow fat climbs the clear hose, joined by food near the end of its digestive journey.

"I could kill you quickly, but after you spent so much time torturing me, not to mention the others, I don't think I will. Besides, I always wondered what would happen if one of these got jammed in someone's lungs."

A hard push, and the tip slices through organs and blood vessels into his left lung. He gasps for breath, fighting the suction but failing. I let him suffer for almost a minute before I pull back and turn the instrument in a new direction.

"Then there's the bladder, Mr. Pickett. I always wondered why you made us call you that. Did it make you feel powerful? In control?" I smile. "Now I'm in control. Ever pissed yourself from the inside?"

The trocar cuts through intestines this time, slicing open the bladder's thin wall and sending yellow liquid up the clear tube. His eyes are wide, and I know he is in pain, close to death but afraid to let himself go. Pulling the trocar back, I position it for a final thrust.

"Ready to bleed out from the inside?" His eyes roll back in his head as I shove the trocar into his chest, the tube filling with rich red blood as the tip finds his heart. Watching the last of the color drain from his face, I pull out the trocar and lay it on the table next to him.

"Good riddance, you old bastard," I mutter.

The fire burns through the night. After dawn, the chief comes to where I'm standing.

"Sorry about the building, Alex," he says. "I didn't realize you owned it."

I nod. "Bought it a few years ago to keep some corporate firm from coming in here."

"Makes sense. We found a car out back; the old owner's. Mr. Pickett. He's had a tough time the last few years; we figure he might have come up here to kill himself last night. Don't know how he did it, if he set the fire then used another method or if he burned himself to death, but his body will be in there, I bet."

"That's horrible," I say, looking at the smoldering remains with practiced concern.

"Yeah. It'll probably end up as a county call, since he lost his money in the recession," the chief says. "Poor man."

"He wasn't the only one," I agree, thinking of the victims I know about, and wondering how many others have taken a painful secret to their graves.

Midnight Train from Toyah

I was the only passenger as the train gathered speed leaving Toyah. Outside, the moon shone bright and full, illuminating the outskirts of the desert town. I hadn't seen the conductor in some time. He was probably back in the caboose with the brakeman, drinking coffee and trying to stay awake.

I'd tried to sleep, but the uncomfortable wooden seats made it hard to drift off. So I stared out at the shadowy shapes on the dark terrain. We were past Toyah now, and all there was to see was flat desert, an occasional mesquite bush or tumbleweed breaking up the monotony.

The train thundered over a ravine, and the moonlight shone off a trickle of water in the bottom. It was the first water I'd seen since the Rio Grande, a hundred and fifty miles behind us.

And on the other side of the Rio Grande, the Federales were wondering where I'd disappeared to after killing two men and stealing a mine payroll.

In the distance, I saw something moving across the desert, barely visible against the dark night. Probably a cowboy working late, I decided.

But instead of fading behind the speeding train, they got closer.

Soon he was riding alongside the coach, his black horse moving in an easy canter. As he pulled his leg across the horse, I realized he intended to jump aboard.

"Wait!" I yelled, but he'd already jumped. I heard him land on the platform at the front of the car. The door swung open, and he stepped inside.

A black cloak covered his body, a black hood hiding his face in shadows. Reaching up, a gloved hand pulled the hood back.

His skin was red; not like a Native, but like a tomato or a rose, a deep color that seemed impossible. His eyes focused on me without needing to look around, and I found myself staring back into black pupils surrounded by yellow irises.

"James Bowdoin?" he asked, his voice a deep rumble that seemed to start in his feet and grow until it burst out his mouth.

I nodded. He took a black metal watch from his cloak pocket and opened it. "It appears I am a few minutes early." A smile. "I'm sure you have questions."

"Are you the devil?" I whispered. He laughed, a deep, rolling laugh that shook the train car.

"Goodness, no. Satan doesn't venture out of hell for anyone less than royalty, though he does take the odd bishop from time to time. I am Lyrn, a demon of the collective order." A gloved hand extended, and after a moment, I shook it.

What the hell do you say when a demon turns up to claim your soul? He was so big, so imposing, I thought I *should* have been scared, but instead I was almost reassured by his presence.

"So, er, collective order, does that mean you're here to…"

"Collect your soul, yes, here in…" The black watch appeared again, and Lyrn studied it. "About two minutes."

Looking out the window, I saw the horse galloping along next to the train. I turned back to Lyrn. "And what is going to happen in about two minutes to make my soul available for collection?"

"Perceptive question." He leaned toward me, and I fought the urge to back away. "Some bandits have mined the track ahead, and the engineer is running a little faster than he should be. So instead of blowing under the engine, it will blow under this car."

"But what if I move cars? If I can make it to the engine, will I survive?"

The red head shook. "No, I'm afraid that's not allowed. Once a soul is claimed, collection can't be avoided."

"But why me? Why now?"

He shrugged. "Your time has come. If it makes you feel better, I'll be returning for one of the bandits shortly."

"Actually, it doesn't." I looked down at the floor.

"Ah, well." The watch appeared again. "Less than a minute now, if there's anything you'd like to say, go ahead and get it out."

I gestured around the car. "It's not like there's anyone to hear me."

"True enough, true enough."

I looked deep into the yellow eyes. "I really don't want to die."

He shrugged again. "Most don't. But it can't be avoided."

I felt the car being lifted from the rails before I heard the explosion. Ahead of us, the whistle shrieked and the brakes squealed. As the car began descending, Lyrn held out a hand. "It's time, James Bowdoin. Come with me."

I wanted to refuse, to fight him, but my hand was already extending, and the demon pulled my soul free. As he led me out of the car, I looked back to see my body slouched in the seat, surrounded by flames.

We leapt from the platform, landing on Lyrn's running horse. The great beast turned away from the crashing train, bounding across the desert at a speed I'd never thought possible.

Faster and faster the horse ran, hooves thundering against the desert floor. Ahead of us, the sky seemed to split apart, the night peeling back to reveal a lake of fire and the sounds of eternal torment.

"Welcome to your new home," Lyrn said from behind me as the horse leapt from the desert into Hell.

Run. Hide. Fight.

It sounded like fireworks, but she knew it wasn't. They were too loud, too close, as Grace jumped off the toilet and pressed her body against the locked door of the bathroom.

They'd done drills for this; no company could avoid them. "Active Shooter Protocol," the laminated page on the bulletin board said. Just beneath it, in big, bold letters, were the words "Run. Hide. Fight."

It had sounded so simple, and the jokes they'd made in the break room after they'd completed the training seemed funny at the time. But now, with screams and gunshots on the other side of the door, they didn't seem funny at all.

Opening the door a crack, she peeked out into the hallway. It was empty. Twenty feet away was an emergency exit. If she could get to it, she could get outside.

Had someone called the police? Her cell phone was on her desk, charging. Surely someone else in the office park had heard the shots. If she could get to the door, she would make sure.

Then she heard the voice booming out of the break room. "Where is Grace?"

The door slid shut and she leaned against it. Andrew. She should have known.

He'd been an accountant here when she started, but his unwelcome advances slowly became more and more disturbing. One night when they were working late, he'd come into her office, closing the door behind him.

"What do you want, Andrew," she asked, wishing he'd left the door open.

"I know you want me," he said, a perverted grin on his face.

"No, I don't." She turned back to the computer, hoping he'd get the message, but the next thing she knew, his arm was wrapping around her.

"Get off of me!" she yelled, turning her chair and pushing him away from her.

He laughed. "I like a little fight in a woman."

Grace got to her feet. "You're not going to like the way I fight."

The perverted grin returned. "Wanna bet?"

At that moment, someone banged on her office door. Before Grace could move toward it, it swung open to reveal their boss, Dennis.

"I heard a commotion; is something wrong?"

"No!" Andrew said.

Grace rolled her eyes. "Yes."

Andrew had been fired on the spot, but it had taken a restraining order to remove him from her life.

Or so she had thought.

She opened the door again, and heard Andrew's voice. "Don't lie to me, Carl! Her car is in the parking lot, and her phone is on her desk!"

"She took my car!" Grace could imagine Carl in the break room, standing between Andrew and the other employees, head up and proud like the former marine he was. Then she heard a gunshot, and Marcia, the receptionist, screamed.

"Anyone else want to lie?" Andrew asked. Grace looked at the exit again, and made a decision. Quietly closing the door behind her, she crawled down the hall away from the exit, toward the break room.

Fuck running and hiding. She'd already done that.

It was time to fight.

The only room between her and the break room was a supply closet, and she slipped inside. Turning on the light, she looked for something, anything, she could use as a weapon. Pencils, pens, notepads, calculators—nothing that would do any kind of damage.

But did she need to hurt him, or just distract him?

She took a box of paper clips and tried the weight in her hand. It would work for what she had in mind. Letting herself out, she crept down the hall and peeked around the break room door.

Carl's body was in the middle of the floor, a pool of blood surrounding his head. At the table in the corner, Marcia and Dennis huddled. Andrew was standing at Carl's feet, his gun aimed at Dennis.

"Where the fuck is she, fat man?" he demanded.

"Are you going to shoot me?" Grace saw his eyes flash red, a hint of the creature lurking within him. Andrew paused, distracted by the change, but not sure what he had seen, and Grace saw her chance.

The box of paper clips exploded as it hit the far wall, the clips rattling as they hit the floor; Andrew spun around and started shooting, but it was too late. Grace leapt over Carl's body and slammed her shoulder into Andrew, driving him into the wall. Calling her true form, she sank her teeth into his neck and ripped away the flesh, tearing open blood vessels. Andrew screamed, keeping his finger on the trigger, but the gun had twisted in his hands, the bullets flying away from them as she held him against the wall. Finally, he went limp, and Grace let his body fall to the floor before turning to look at the table.

Marcia was dead, hit by the last wild rounds. Dennis picked up his coffee and took a sip. "Took you long enough."

The wolf standing over Andrew's body rolled her eyes. "You could have done something," she said, reverting to her human disguise.

"I didn't have a chance without revealing myself to Carl and Marcia. Didn't matter in the end though," he said, a small note of sadness in his voice as he looked at the bodies of their former coworkers. "That's the challenge of working with humans."

"I should have killed him the night he assaulted me," Grace growled, glaring at the body slumped against the wall.

Dennis put a hand on her shoulder. "You didn't want to blow your cover. At the time, it made sense." He took an ice pick from the top of the refrigerator and poked it into Andrew's wounds, making sure to get blood on the blade and handle. Then he reached for the phone on the wall.

"911... Yes, there's been an active shooter incident at our business... No, the shooter is dead... Nacyl Accounting Associates on Bedford... Thank you..."

Grandma's Advice

Eighty thousand fans roared as the Tigers ran into the stadium, led by orange-and-black-clad cheerleaders as the marching band thundered the school's fight song. When they reached the sideline, the cheers turned to boos as their rivals, the Falcons, ran onto the opposite end of the field.

"You ready?" Dane Kelly, the Tigers' offensive coordinator, asked his quarterback.

"Yeah." Grabbing a ball off the bench, Vic Hoffman faked a throw into the stands, earning cheers from a group of girls sitting a few rows up.

"Not still thinking about that girl, are you?"

Hoffman sighed. "Look, it was consensual. She just hates athletes, and when she found out I was on the football team, she made up a story saying she was raped."

Kelly held up his hands. "I ain't accusing you, buddy. I believe you."

"Good, 'cuz a lot of folks don't."

He clapped Hoffman on his shoulder pads. "Those folks don't matter right now. Just go out there and play the game."

The Falcons got the ball first and went three-and-out, punting the ball to the Tigers. Hoffman trotted onto the field.

"Red 33 Flag Sweep," he told the other players when he reached the huddle. With a clap of their hands, they broke to their positions, Hoffman taking his behind the center.

Looking left and right to make sure his team was in position, he got ready to take the ball. "Down! Set!" he yelled, checking the defense for surprise changes.

Blue eyes stared back at him. The defensive lineman's head was gone, replaced by a blonde young woman's.

"Why did you rape me, Vic?"

"I didn't!"

The ball was jammed into his hands as the center charged forward. Vic managed to corral it, turning to see the fullback rushing to take the handoff. Vic blinked for a moment; the fullback's head had turned into the blonde woman's. Then the man was past him, and Vic still had the ball.

Controlled violence had erupted around him as the offensive line fought to keep the defense at bay. Vic saw a big, blue-jerseyed defender get free and run toward him. Vic turned away and crashed into another blue-clad player who threw him to the ground.

"That's what you deserve," a female voice said as blue eyes looked down at him. Then the Falcon turned away, and she was gone.

"You okay, Vic?" Eddie Leonard, the fullback, offered a hand to help him up.

"Yeah." He looked over at the defense. Eleven ugly football players. No blonde girl in sight.

"Get your head in it, man," Eddie said, slapping his pads as they reached the huddle.

"19 Fly Wasp Bravo," he called, comparing the coach's signal to his wristband. They broke huddle and lined up, Vic standing behind the center in shotgun formation.

"Down! Set!"

This time it was the middle linebacker turning blonde and staring back at him with accusing blue eyes. "You had no right," she said. "Being a football star doesn't mean you can fuck anyone you want."

"Go away!"

The ball flew toward him and bounced off his fingertips. Vic fell on it, and heard the whistle ending the play.

Getting to his feet, he heard another whistle and saw the referee signaling for a timeout. Trotting to the sideline, he looked up at the stands and froze.

Thousands of blonde faces stared down at him, blue eyes piercing his soul. This wasn't fair. She was ruining his game, his life.

"You deserve this, asshole!" thousands of voices roared in unison, forcing him to cover his ears. "Was it worth it?"

Hoffman fell to his knees. "Stop it! Stop it, please!" he sobbed, as three more Bekahs ran toward him from the sideline. "No! No!"

"It looks like something is wrong with Tiger Quarterback Vic Hoffman."

"Jake, he hasn't looked like himself this first drive, and with the way he's acting now, you have to wonder if Andre Lisbon hit him harder than we thought back on first down."

A phone rang, and the volume on the television was muted.

"Hello?" A blonde-haired, blue-eyed girl leaned back in her chair. The apartment was a mile from the stadium, but she could still hear the PA announcer's voice through the closed window.

"Hey Grandma," she said, fiddling with the charm of her necklace. "Bekah" was spelled out in flowing gold script. "You saw? I think he's learning an important lesson. Thanks for the advice."

Bekah looked down at a box on the table, where a plastic doll in an orange jersey was surrounded by hundreds of pictures of her smiling face.

Consumed

"**M**org, all I'm saying is there's a reason this place was abandoned." Ellie swept a cobweb from the eaves. "Cabin built, well dug, land plowed, and no sign of anyone."

"Hey," Morgan said, walking over to embrace her. "Don't look a gift horse in the mouth. This is everything we need, and with you close to bursting." His hand dropped to her stomach. "Any time I don't have to waste building a shelter and clearing fields is a blessing."

She smiled up at him. "Okay, Morg." Her hand moved on top of his. "We still need to decide on names."

"Soon," Morgan said, taking the broom from her. "You've done enough today; you need to rest."

Ellie woke in the night to find Morgan sitting by the fire. "Everything alright?"

"What?" He looked up. "Oh, yeah. Just trying to decide what I need to get done tomorrow."

"Can't you do it in bed? It's kind of cold without you."

He sighed, almost like she was annoying him. "I'll be there in a minute." Morgan returned his gaze to the glowing embers as she rolled over.

The next day was a flurry of activity. They unloaded the wagon, moving the rest of their belongings inside. After making some repairs to the split-rail fence, Morgan moved the oxen into the corral behind the house. By the time night fell, their work and the smell of stew and corn cakes drifting from the hearth had transformed the cabin into a home.

Ellie woke to find Morgan sitting in front of the fire again, staring into the embers. Climbing out of bed, she padded across the floor, putting a hand on his shoulder.

"Jesus, Ellie, you scared me."

"Sorry," she said. "Just saw you sitting here alone and wondered what you were doing."

"Not much. Just thinking."

"About the baby?"

"Yeah, I guess." He looked up at her, and she leaned down and kissed him.

"It'll be okay, Morg." She rubbed his back, and he looked up at her, the flames reflecting in his eyes. "You coming back to bed?"

"In a minute, babe."

With a squeeze of his shoulder, she went back to bed.

Morgan was working outside when he saw a lone rider coming across the prairie. As the man approached the cabin, he forked his horse, and Morgan could see the gold star pinned to his shirt.

"You're not Wayne Jessup," the lawman opened.

Morgan shook his head. "We're the Kitwells. Just came out from Alabama."

He raised an eyebrow. "No one was here when you got here?"

Morgan shook his head. "The place was abandoned. Nothing inside or out."

"And that didn't seem strange?"

Morgan shrugged. "Life's hard out here, figured whoever was here just couldn't hack it. I was planning to come into town once we got settled to look into things. My wife's in the family way, so finding a place already built like this was a blessing."

The sheriff looked toward the cabin door, and Morgan turned to see Ellie standing there.

"Howdy," she called, walking out to them.

"Well, hello." The lawman touched the brim of his hat. "I'm Sheriff Pittman."

"Ellie Kitwell. I just finished making lunch if you'd like to join us, Sheriff."

He shook his head. "I appreciate the offer, but I've got to get back to town. I just stopped to check in on the Jessups." The Sheriff looked out across the prairie, then finally back at Morgan. "Reckon I should tell you, y'all are the fifth family to occupy this cabin since

Sam Waller built it two years ago. The last four up and vanished, leaving nothing but the cabin behind."

Morgan nodded. "I appreciate you telling us, Sheriff. Like I said, it's a rough life out here."

The sheriff looked at the house, then spit tobacco juice in the dirt. "If I was you, I'd get out, go someplace else. Just a thought." He touched his hat. "You folks have a nice day. Hopefully we'll see each other again."

"Should we go?" Ellie asked as they watched the sheriff ride away.

Morgan laughed. "It sounds like something made up to scare folks. Just because those other families couldn't hack it doesn't mean we can't."

She put her hand on his arm. "I know. But with the baby coming, I worry, Morg."

He leaned down and kissed her. "Ain't nothing going to happen, Ellie. This is our home now."

She smiled. "I like that word. Home."

Ellie woke to find Morgan staring at a roaring fire, the flames licking up the chimney past the mantle.

"Morgan, what the hell!" She jumped out of bed, but stopped when he turned toward her.

Flames were dancing in his eyes. "It's beautiful, Ellie," he said, his voice deeper than she'd ever heard it.

Ellie shook her head. "It's just fire, Morg. We gotta put it out before it burns the place down."

"No, Ellie," a smile crept across his face, the flames still in his eyes. "This fire is a blessing, just like this cabin. It can consume us, give us everything we could ever want."

She thought back to the dust she'd swept up the first day. Now that she thought about it, it had looked a lot like ash.

Ellie looked across the cabin to the door, and a hand shot out and grabbed her.

"Come with me, Ellie. Join me, join us, in the fire."

Yanking her arm away, she backed away from Morgan as the flames danced even higher. His eyes never left her, almost seeming to burn her with their intensity.

"Are you leaving, Ellie?"

She nodded.

"We can't have that."

Ellie turned and ran as Morgan laughed behind her. As she reached for the door, the flames swept over her body, consuming her.

Nostalgia

B illy opened the clubhouse door and stepped inside.

Using his phone's flashlight, he walked past the empty lockers to the manager's office. He'd spent hours in here as a kid, watching his dad run the Green Sox, the best minor league baseball team anywhere.

Even with spending hours around some great players, Billy hadn't been athletic enough for a baseball career. His degree was in business, and he'd done well. So well that he'd come home and bought the Sox.

Now they were moving out of the old Green Sox Stadium, into a modern park downtown. Billy had decided to come back one last time before the demolition crews began, to spend some time alone with his memories.

His reflection was interrupted by the crack of a bat.

"What the fuck?" He walked toward the dugout tunnel. Probably some damn kids, ruining his moment with the old place.

As he reached the top of the tunnel, he saw two men standing on the field.

"Hey Little Boss," a muscular young man called from the batter's box. On the mound, the other man tossed a ball toward the plate, and the batter swung, launching the ball over the advertisement-covered outfield wall.

"Damn it, Mickey," the pitcher called, staring out at the landing spot. "You didn't have to show me up like that!"

"Guess you should've pitched better, then."

"You're dead!" Billy yelled, walking onto the field. "Both of you!" Mickey had been killed leaving the stadium, a robbery gone wrong. The pitcher, Avery, had taken a beanball to the head, dying in the batter's box as Billy and five thousand horrified fans watched.

"Well, you're right," Avery said, another ball appearing in his hand. He wound up and fired. Mickey brought the bat around, slicing a wicked grounder down the third base line.

"Better!" he called to Avery.

"What the fuck are you doing here?" Billy demanded.

"Stopping a mistake." Mickey stepped out of the box toward him. "You gotta save this place, Little Boss."

Billy had forgotten Mickey used to call him that, just like he'd called his dad "Big Boss." He shook his head. "This place is old, Mickey, past its prime."

"You're wrong, Little Boss," Avery called.

"Look around," Mickey said, waving his hand toward the covered grandstand. "It's just reaching its prime!"

"No luxury boxes or videoboard, basic concessions, plumbing and sewer problems every night; hell, we still have troughs for urinals!" Billy shook his head. "This place is the oldest park in the league by fifty years, and it shows!"

"Which is what makes it great." Avery had come in from the mound to join them. "When a little boy sings 'Take Me Out to the Ballgame,' this is the kind of place he's thinking about, a place where he can sit in the bleachers and visit with the bullpen."

"And you don't need a fancy concession stand," Mickey added. "Just Cracker Jacks and those nachos with the gooey orange cheese. No luxury boxes, just a simple scoreboard that tells you who's winning. That's where the magic is."

"There's no money in magic though," Billy protested.

"You've got enough damn money, kid," Avery said. "You've done well. But keeping this place around is about more than money. It's an investment in a better world."

"Ain't no other place like it," Mickey agreed. "It may be wood and concrete, but the memories holding it together make it so much more. And you want to knock it down?"

Billy shrugged. "It's prime real estate."

"It's prime real estate now," Avery shot back. "Torn down it's nothing more than a place selling cheap shit no one needs, or luxury housing no one can afford!"

"Your dad understood that, Little Boss," Mickey said. "He'd have never torn this place down."

Billy clenched his fists. "How dare you bring Dad into this? How dare you use him to further your agenda? He's been dead ten years! How could you know what he would want?"

"We're dead too, kid," Avery said. "If you'd ever visited that shithole nursing home where you stuck him the last few years of his life, he might have told you himself. But you didn't, so now it's on us."

"Look, nostalgia is great, but seriously, this place is a money pit! It barely breaks even!" Billy shook his head. "Dad never understood the business side of things."

"Because he understood something more important," Mickey said. "The human side of things!"

"It doesn't matter," Billy snarled. "This place is history! Next year, the Green Sox will have a new home!"

"With some fancy corporate name someone pays you a couple million bucks for, right?" Avery asked as another ball appeared in his hand. "Since it doesn't look like we can talk you out of this, how about you take a couple swings before you go, for old time's sake."

With a sigh, Billy nodded. "Yeah. That's the kind of nostalgia I can go for."

Mickey handed him the bat, and he walked to home plate. Taking his place on the mound, Avery went into his wind-up.

The pitch hit Billy just above the ear, knocking him to the dirt. The bat rolled away, coming to a stop in front of Mickey.

"Jesus! Fuck!" Billy yelled, holding his hands to his head and feeling the blood flowing beneath them.

A shadow crossed him, and he looked up.

"Hate to do this, Little Boss," Mickey said, raising the bat. "But you didn't leave us a choice."

Monster of the Chamber

I found my spot at the window of the steel chamber, watching the man being strapped to the metal chair inside. He seemed calm, incapable of the nine brutal murders that had terrorized Mayfield the previous summer.

Next to me was Grady Clevenger, the cop who finally tracked the killer down. He shook his head as the warden stepped into the chamber.

"I didn't think we'd end up here," Clevenger said as the warden read the death warrant. "It took five shots to put him down. Hell, three of the bullets are still in him!"

"Tough sonuvabitch," I agreed as the warden left the chamber. The metal door closed with a satisfying slam.

"Yeah. At least tonight we'll finish what I started."

"Ladies and Gentlemen," the warden said, his voice echoing off the stone walls of the room. "The execution of J.T. Edmonds is about to begin. As warden of the state penitentiary, I will be carrying out the sentence of the court. I asked Mr. Edmonds if he had a final statement, and he responded, 'no.'"

The warden looked once at a phone against the wall. Even though it was my first time witnessing an execution, I knew it was the direct line to the Governor. When it didn't ring, the warden reached out and pulled a lever attached to the side of the chamber.

A white mist slowly filled the inside, clouding my view of Edmonds. Cyanide gas. He coughed once, twice, then his head slumped forward, resting on his chest.

"Damn peaceful way to go," Clevenger muttered. "Not like his victims."

I silently agreed with him. The murders had started just after I arrived to work for the newspaper in Mayfield, young women being abducted from the town and found slashed to death near the railyard.

For a while, women would barely look at a man they didn't know, ruining my dating life. It had upset me, until I was sent to cover a new victim who had been found. The body was lying in a pool of blood, deep slashes carved into her skin, the spine the only thing keeping her head attached to her torso.

"Something's wrong," Clevenger said, snapping me out of my reverie.

In the chamber, Edmonds's fair skin had gone pale white. His hair was growing, changing from dark brown to white. He lifted his head, his red eyes glowing among the gas.

Something hit the window, and I realized it was the buckle of one of the straps holding Edmonds to the chair. Another followed, his muscles expanding and pushing through the leather.

"What about the cyanide?" I asked.

"I don't know," Clevenger stammered. "I've never seen anything like this. He should be fucking dead!"

In the chamber, Edmonds stood, and the diminutive man I'd seen strapped to the chair was gone.

In his place was a monster, almost as tall as the chamber's ceiling, muscles rippling as he stomped around the room.

When he got to my window, he stopped. "Clevenger!"

The veteran cop stepped back from the window. The area around the gas chamber had emptied, leaving only us and the warden. As I watched, Edmonds ripped the chair out of the floor. He slammed it into the window, sending a spiderweb of cracks through it.

"Run!" The warden yelled. "If the glass breaks, we'll be exposed to the gas!"

I was diving through the door when a crash told me Edmonds had broken the glass. Rolling to the side, I huddled next to the steps, looking up at the door and waiting.

I heard a scream from inside, followed by thundering footsteps. Scooting away, I wished myself invisible.

Clevenger's body came out first, held up by a massive set of razor-sharp claws. Edmonds didn't bother to duck, smashing through the stonework and leaving a hole that extended three feet above the door frame.

"Mother of God," I whispered, as Edmonds turned toward me.

"Going somewhere?"

I nodded, continuing to back away from him. An alarm sounded, and spotlights from the guard tower focused on the death house door. He looked away, roaring at the lights, flinging Clevenger's body into the blinding beams.

Turning back toward me, he covered a third of the ground between us in a single step.

Death was coming, in the form of this mutated vision of hell.

A gunshot rang out, and the beast put a hand to his shoulder. Turning, he roared at the tower, an unearthly, booming noise that seemed to start at his feet and build until it flooded out of his mouth.

Then the wall behind him began to spark, and a machine gun thundered, drowning out the roar. Edmonds swiped at the air like he was trying to bat away the bullets, but as another gun entered the fight, he sank to his knees, then crashed to the ground.

I sat huddled in the shadows as the guards came running. The warden stumbled out of the death house, a bloody gash on his arm soaking his shirt, blood dripping off his hand onto the cement steps.

Two guards helped me to my feet and tried to lead me toward the gate, but I pulled away from them and approached Edmonds. Grabbing his hair, I lifted the head and stared into the glowing red eyes before they faded to darkness.

"The execution of J.T. Edmonds has been carried out," the warden gasped, before collapsing into the arms of a guard.

Tattoos and Scars

I got my first tattoo when I was sixteen.

A couple of friends and I snuck out and painted the town's water tower. The usual childish bullshit, Principal Murphy's phone number and "call for a good time" in bright red letters. We thought it would make us legends.

Chief Larsen was waiting at the bottom of the ladder when we climbed down the tower.

"How original," he said, shining his light up at the tower. His squad car was parked nearby, and the trunk was open. He pointed to it. "White paint's in there. I don't want to see a speck of red when you're done."

My father was waiting at the door as Larsen marched me up the driveway, my clothes splattered in red and white paint.

"You should have cuffed him," Dad said.

Larsen shrugged. "He's just a fool kid."

"A fool kid who needs the fear of God put into him." Dad crossed his arms and looked down at me, the porch adding to his height and making me feel small. "Get in this house, young man!"

I sat at the kitchen table and laid my head on my arms. Soon, Dad came in.

"Vandalism? Jesus, Ross! You're gonna have to go before the judge and everything! Your mother is probably rolling over in her grave right now!"

My mother. Every time I did something wrong, her ghost appeared. "I'm just glad your mother isn't alive to see this." "Your mother would be so embarrassed." It felt like she had been perfect, except for giving birth to a screw-up like me.

"Well!" Dad demanded. "What do you have to say for yourself?"

"Nothing," I muttered, not even bothering to lift my head.

"Nothing?" Dad grabbed a handful of my hair and lifted my head off the table. "The police chief brings you home, and all you have to say is 'nothing?'"

"What the fuck do you want me to say? I thought Mom wasn't getting enough exercise, and spinning in her grave might do her some good?"

He let go, glaring down at me. "You'll pay for that."

"I don't care!" I laid my head back on the table.

Dad slammed his head down next to my head, and I jumped.

"Do I have your attention?"

"Sure. Whatever."

He shook his head. "You know better than to act like this, son. And I'm gonna make sure you never forget what you learned tonight."

"Right arm or left?"

Dad had called me down to his tattoo parlor, and sat me down in one of the chairs.

"What?"

He held out a stencil, and I gulped.

It was a water tower.

"Right arm or left?"

I shook my head. "I don't want it."

"I don't give a damn. You need to remember there's consequences to your actions." He pulled over a tray of equipment and sat down next to me.

"It's my body, and I don't want a tattoo!" I protested.

"It wasn't your water tower, and you saw fit to vandalize it. Right arm or left?"

I sighed. "Right."

The tattoo needle fucking hurt as Dad moved it around my arm. I looked away, not wanting to see what he was doing. I'd never wanted a tattoo.

Now I was being punished with one.

When he finished, Dad examined his work with a smile. "I don't reckon you'll ever make a mistake like that again, huh, Ross?"

I made more mistakes.

Six months later, a script "liar" was added under the water tower. I'd told him I'd gone bowling, but he found me smoking pot by the creek.

A year after that, three months before my eighteenth birthday, I got another. This time, it was a car with a skeleton in the driver's seat.

That wasn't fair.

The accident hadn't been my fault.

But the other driver died, and I got the tattoo.

The day after I turned eighteen, I went to a lawyer's office to sign some paperwork for Mom's estate. She'd left me some money for college, and I intended to go as far from my dad as I could get.

Alaska, maybe.

"And this is for the victim's fund from the state," the lawyer said, pushing a piece of paper across the desk.

"What?" I shook my head. "Mom died in a car accident."

The lawyer narrowed his brow in confusion. "No, it was a shooting."

"What?"

He pulled a faded newspaper clipping from the file and slid it across the desk. I picked it up and read, the first sentence jumping out at me.

Twenty-three year old Marla Ridges was assaulted and killed Friday when three men came to her home looking to settle her husband's drug debts.

I looked down at the tattoos on my arms, feeling my temper rising.

I was an embarrassment to Mom?

At least I hadn't put her in her grave.

Dad was going to pay.

That night, I waited until I heard him snoring before slipping into his bedroom.

He was lying on his back, shirtless, his entire body covered in tattoos except for his chest. Dad told everyone he was saving it for his Mona Lisa, waiting for the perfect idea to come to him.

It had come to me instead, sitting there in that lawyer's office.

Raising the paring knife in my hand, I hoped the sleeping pills I'd slipped into his beer would keep him unconscious.

Pressing the tip into the skin above his right nipple, I slashed down.

He snorted, but didn't wake.

My work wasn't neat. Quick slashes with the small knife, blood pooling on his skin and blocking my view. But as I used a blanket to wipe the blood away, I was proud of my work.

"Liar" was carved into my father's chest.

Setting a copy of the article from the lawyer's file on the bedside table, I slipped out of the house, wondering which of my tattoos I should remove first.

Ghost Flight

Terry Kilgore pulled back on the yoke and his plane lifted off the runway of Greeneville's airport. It was a beautiful summer afternoon, not a cloud in the sky, and he could feel the energy start to return to his body. He needed this.

The world's problems fell away with the ground. The loss of his wife, the two grandchildren who had been in the car with her when she had the heart attack. His granddaughter had passed in the wreck, and his grandson was still in the hospital. His daughter had made it clear she didn't hold him responsible, but he still felt guilty. His wife, his car; why wouldn't he feel guilty?

Well, he'd felt guilty on the ground.

Passing through five thousand feet, he turned east to fly along the mountains. He loved being able to look out across the green peaks.

Above him, he saw an airliner crossing his path. That was odd; it was low for an airliner in these parts. He reached for the radio.

"Tri-Cities, this is Echo-Whiskey-Four inquiring about traffic in my area of operation."

It took a minute, but the voice came back. "Echo-Whiskey, Tri-Cities, we show you with fifteen miles clear in all directions."

Fifteen miles? That couldn't be right, he thought, turning to follow the airliner. "Ah, Tri-cities, Echo-Whiskey, is that based on scope or reports?" In other words, were they looking at the radar, or just relying on where the planes said they were?

"Echo-Whiskey, Tri-cities, I am looking at the scope, it's actually a bit more than fifteen miles. Is something wrong?"

Kilgore grabbed his binoculars for a closer look. It was an older aircraft; it looked like a Vickers, but it had "United" clearly painted on the side. "Tri-cities, Echo-Whiskey, I have an older airliner in sight, estimate altitude at ten thousand, range less than ten miles. Passing east of Greeneville right now on a South-Southwest heading."

The radio was silent for almost a minute as Terry moved his plane to follow the airliner. It was descending slowly, headed toward Newport. Finally his headset crackled back to life.

"Ah, Echo-Whiskey, we have no reports of commercial traffic in your area, or anything on radar to suggest there is an aircraft there. Are you sure of what you're looking at?"

Terry yanked off his headset and threw it in the passenger seat. What the fuck did they think, he was calling for shits and giggles? Pushing his throttles forward, he closed the distance to the second plane as he fished for the headset using its cable. As he pulled it on his head, a voice came again.

"Echo-Whiskey, tri-cities, I think we lost you."

"Roger, tri-cities, Echo-Whiskey, had some headset trouble. I've closed the gap and can confirm the airplane I'm looking at is an older-model Vickers airliner, with United markings." Terry looked at the plane again. It was still descending, awfully fast now. Then he saw the orange light in the windows. "Tri-cities, Echo-Whiskey, that Vickers is on fire!"

"Echo-Whiskey, this is Foxtrot-Bravo, report position?"

Terry sighed. Foxtrot-Bravo was his friend, Dave Morgan. "Foxtrot-Bravo, this is Echo-Whiskey. We're crossing the Nolichuckey at the 107 bridge."

"Terry, I just lifted off from Morristown, heading your way. We'll get to the bottom of this."

"Foxtrot-Bravo, Tri-cities, please use proper radio etiquette on this channel." Terry rolled his eyes. Proper radio etiquette be damned, that plane was going down.

"Tri-cities, Echo-Whiskey, the Vickers is turning south, headed toward the French Broad," Terry reported, turning his own plane to follow.

A new voice came on the line. "Echo-Whiskey, Tri-cities, I don't know what the hell you're up to, but there is no plane where you say there is. Now you need to clear this channel for real traffic, and you better hope we don't figure out who you are, because the fines for a false report are steep..."

"Goddammit Tri-cities," Terry exploded. "I'm watching this plane go down, it's on fire, and I don't know why you won't get your head out of your ass and figure out what's going on!"

"Echo-Whiskey, Foxtrot-Bravo. Terry, I'm crossing the lake at White Pine. Hang tight, buddy. We'll figure it out."

The plane in front of him was starting to drop. It was headed toward a low ridge, just north of Parrottsville, and it was about to crash. "Hurry up, Dave, she's fading quick. She won't be airborne when you get here."

"Clear this channel!" Tri-cities roared. "Be advised, we are opening an investigation into illegal use of FAA frequencies..."

"Go stuff your head," Terry shot back. The flames were visible outside the cabin now, as the pilots fought to keep the Vickers in the air. Terry saw the plane barely clear a low barn before crashing into the hillside. A fireball lifted above the wreck.

"Tri-cities, Echo-Whiskey, the Vickers is down, approximately two miles north of Parrottsville!" Terry said, passing over the wreck site. Turning his plane, he saw Dave approaching from the northwest. Coming out of the turn, he flew back over the wreck site to find... Nothing.

"Echo-Whiskey, Foxtrot-Bravo. I don't see anything."

"It was just there," Terry whispered. "I swear it was."

"Echo-Whiskey, Tri-Cities, expect an investigation over this," the angry voice of the supervisor growled.

"I swear I saw it," Terry said, as the memory ran through his mind. The plane roaring over the top of the barn before plummeting into the hillside.

"Echo-Whiskey, this is Alpha-Alpha. Say, do you know what day it is?"

What the fuck? "Alpha-Alpha, Echo-Whiskey. It's the Ninth of July."

"Ah," the voice came again. "Echo-Whiskey, Alpha-Alpha, I think you done saw the Ghost of United Flight 823. Went down outside Parrottsville over fifty years ago. Saw it myself nine years ago."

"A ghost?" Terry circled again, looking down at the unblemished landscape.

"It's alright," Dave said over the radio. "Could have happened to anyone."

"But it didn't," Terry said, thinking about the face he'd seen in the plane's window.

His grandson's face.

Counting Spoons

T his is not my bed.

I'm sure I fell asleep in my bed, in my apartment near the university.

But this is not my bed.

A pair of flickering fluorescent bulbs light the room, with no windows to tell me what time it is or show me where I am. It's a small room, and I don't see anything but the bed I'm lying on. There isn't even a light switch, or a knob on the door.

I swing my legs off the bed and my foot hits a bucket on the floor. Someone has taped a label to it: "toilet." Cute.

I realize I need to pee, and move the bucket to a corner before making use of it. Looking around, I don't see a camera or any other way to monitor me. That doesn't mean there isn't one.

Under the bed sit several gallon jugs of water and a box labeled "MREs–variety."

Where the hell am I?

A hiss of air gets my attention, and I pull out the box of food. There's an air vent under the bed, blowing a cool breeze into the room. That's nice, even if it is too small for me to escape through.

I open one of the jugs and take a swig of water. Then I start thinking.

I'm boring, just a college student who works as a waiter to pay his way through school. If I have any free time, I'm in the library studying or tossing a frisbee around the disc golf course.

Why would someone kidnap me?

I lie down on the bed and stare at the ceiling. It's as white as the rest of the room. No water stains or anything that might distract me from the situation. Just the hiss of air through the vent.

I wake up in the same room as before. I hadn't planned to sleep, but I'd lain down, and the next thing I knew, I was waking up.

The box of rations is still on the floor, and I pull off the tape. "Chili Mac," the one on top says. I pull open the wax paper wrapper and dump the contents onto the bed. Several smaller packets tumble out, each labeled with their contents. "Main course," "Side dish," "Dessert," and others. There are instructions inside, and I use the heating pouch to warm up the main course.

It isn't bad. Better than the college cafeteria, at least.

After I eat, I lie down on my bed. Curious, I tap the wall, but no response comes. It sounds solid though, and feels like it might be concrete under the plaster. I guess I am alone here, wherever I am.

I take the spoon from my meal and lay it on the floor at the foot of the bed. I'll use it to try to keep track of how long I've been here. If only my captor had left me something to pass the time.

I climb to the floor and look under the bed again. Nothing. No books, no paper, nothing to keep me occupied. Just me and an empty room.

There are nine spoons at the foot of the bed now, though I've slept more times than that. Without exercise, I think my body is going into a type of hibernation, passing the time with sleep. Without a window, meals are the only way to guess how long I've been here.

That and the rapidly filling bucket in the corner. It's starting to smell like when I pass the town sewage plant.

Boredom is the worst of it. There's only so far imagination can take you, and I've spent a lot of time sitting on the edge of the bed staring at the door. Is anyone out there looking for me? Surely by now my roommate has noticed my absence, my professors too. If not them, my boss at the restaurant has. Would they tell the police? Or would they assume I'd just stopped coming to class, stopped coming to work, and given up on the life I'd built.

I hope someone misses me, but I'm scared no one does.

Seventeen spoons at the foot of the bed now, and only seven meals left in the MRE box. I wonder if I should have rationed the food out more, but I also know I eat so rarely, it would be hard to limit myself more than I have.

I spend most of my time in bed, wishing for something to do. You can only read the back of an MRE packet so many times, after all.

Who would hate me enough to do this? It's a torture so simple, it has to be a mastermind. But what's the end game? Am I going to run out of food and waste away to nothing? Or will the door open and the answers reveal themselves? It's too much to think about, and I lie down for another nap.

Twenty-three spoons now. In the corner, my toilet is filled to the brim and the room smells like shit. The next meal will be the last one in the box. "Chicken Fajita," the pouch says. I decide to take a nap before I eat it.

I wake up in my own bed.

The sun peeks through the window, shining on my Def Leppard poster on the far wall.

Was it all a dream?

I swing my feet off the bed and they crash into something. Looking down, I see an empty bucket with a small sign taped on it that says "toilet."

In the bottom is an MRE with "Chicken Fajita" printed on the package, and twenty-three plastic spoons.

Beast of the Rappahannock

A LONZO

"Another night on picket duty," Alonzo said, staring into the darkness as he leaned against a tree. To his left, the Rappahannock River flowed by, the moving water barely audible over the crickets. In the woods around them, fireflies blinked among the trees.

"Don't know why we need a picket here," John, his partner, said, sitting on a large rock. "All the Rebs are on the other side of the army."

Alonzo chuckled. "Bobby Lee has a bad habit of showing up where the generals least expect him."

"Damn generals," John muttered. "If they'd get out of our way, we'd win this war."

"I heard Grant is coming east," Alonzo said.

John grunted. "I'll believe it when I see it. Until then, we're stuck with Old Snapping Turtle in command."

"Meade won at Gettysburg," Alonzo reminded him.

"And hasn't done a damn thing since." Getting to his feet, John looked around. Their night vision had settled in now, and the light of a half-moon let them see reasonably well. "I'm gonna go take a piss."

"Alright." Alonzo watched his friend disappear up the trail.

A noise behind Alonzo made him jump. "Damn it, John, you scared me."

By the time he remembered John had gone in the other direction, powerful fingers had a grasp on his arms. He screamed as he was dragged down the embankment to the river. Twisting his body, he tried to break free, and the creature gripped him tighter, sharp fingernails tearing into the flesh of his arms. He felt cold water on his feet and heard splashing. Summoning the last of his strength, he pulled loose, twisting as he fell into the dark river.

Sputtering, he broke the surface and saw the monster. It stood eight feet tall, at least, with long, skinny fingers extending from webbed hands. Scales covered its skin, and gills stuck out of the creature's long neck. It turned its head, twisting from left to right as if it heard something.

Then it dove into the water, and Alonzo felt those thin fingers wrap around his arms and drag him under.

Holding his breath, he tried to kick free, but the beast pulled him deeper. His lungs burned, and he finally had to inhale. Water rushed into his lungs, and the murky water faded to darkness.

JOHN

John had heard his friend scream. Racing to button his pants, he ran back toward where he'd left Alonzo.

His friend was gone. There were marks in the dirt that looked like something had been dragged toward the river. Picking up his musket, he studied the water's surface. Ripples bloomed across it, but he saw no sign of his friend. Glancing around the woods, every shadow seemed to be an enemy: a rebel, a monster, something waiting to treat him like it had Alonzo.

He should sound the alarm, alert the sergeant and the other troops back at the camp, but he wanted to be sure of what had happened. Maybe Alonzo had just fallen in the river and the current had carried him away. His friend could be making his way back up the riverbank now, dripping wet and mad as a hornet.

A webbed hand clamped over John's mouth, preventing him from screaming. But he still had the musket, and he squeezed the trigger.

A bright flash lit the night, the explosive roar disorienting both John and the creature. John dropped the gun, but managed to pull his bayonet out. Rushing the creature, he stabbed it in the leg, earning a howl of pain. Strong hands grabbed John and hurled him down the embankment to the river. He heard a thud as the thing landed next to him; felt the long fingers wrap around his throat and lift him off the ground.

John heard splashing as the creature entered the water, then felt himself being pulled under. Twisting, he broke free for a moment, and as the long fingers reached for him, he grabbed two and pulled them apart, feeling the webbing between them tear apart, slick blood pouring from the wound. Then the other hand closed around his neck and pushed him to the rocky bottom of the river.

He kicked and struggled, silt rising from the river floor and swirling around them.

But the webbed hand still squeezed, the long fingers cutting into his skin. With a final effort, John tried to push off the bottom, only to be slammed back down. As his back hit the rocks, it felt like his soul was forced from his body to be carried away by the muddy water.

THE LIEUTENANT

"What the hell happened?" The lieutenant raised a lantern, studying the scene. A peaceful night of sleep had been interrupted, first by a gunshot, then his sergeant coming to report two missing pickets. "Is Bobby Lee crawling up our ass?"

"If it was Rebs, they wouldn't have made off with two privates," the sergeant said. "They'd have kept coming and we'd have woken to a gunfight."

The lieutenant sighed and looked out at the river. "What about desertion?"

"There's signs of a struggle." The sergeant pointed at the marks in the dirt and the blood-covered bayonet. "It's almost dawn. Probably best to post guards and investigate in the daylight."

"Agreed. You can handle that, Sergeant?"

"Of course."

"Then I'm going back to bed."

The sergeant watched the officer walk away and shook his head. "Useless ass," he muttered before turning to organize the men.

THE BEAST

In the river, the Beast of the Rappahannock slid along under the surface, watching the man with the lantern walk back to camp. He'd eaten well tonight, but the hunger still lingered. His leg hurt too, from where he'd been stabbed.

But he could ignore the pain. It was time to hunt.

As the lieutenant stopped to light a cigar, the beast emerged from the river, creeping up the slope and approaching the officer from behind.

His stomach growled in anticipation as he extended his hands toward the man's neck.

Retort

Darkness. Crowded darkness.

Andrew was lying down on something hard, duct tape wrapped around his hands. He tried to push his arms up, but something was in the way. The lid yielded a little, but not enough for him to see out.

He tried to kick, but he couldn't move his legs.

They were numb.

What had happened to them?

From the texture and smell, he could tell his prison was made of cardboard.

An engine rumbled, and he was moving. So he was in a vehicle of some kind. Around him, he could hear other cars zooming by.

"Hey!" he yelled. "Let me out!"

Laughter came from somewhere above his head. "Holler all you want. Ain't no one going to hear you. And you ain't going nowhere with that little injection I gave you."

That's what had happened to his legs. "Look, man. I don't know who you are, but we can make a deal..."

More laughter. "I done made my deal. Now you best prepare yourself."

"Prepare myself?"

"For the retort."

He'd been downtown, at one of the motels off Dixie Avenue. The whore hadn't told him her name, but she'd been cheap. When they were done, he'd gotten in his car, and that was the last thing he remembered.

"You're gonna die, son," the voice from the front said. "Get right with Jesus while you still can."

Andrew screamed, rocking his body in the confined space, but going nowhere. The laughter from the front got louder.

"That don't sound like praying," his captor called over the scream.

"Fuck you!"

"You're gonna die with profanity on your lips? Maybe you ain't gonna see the Lord at all. Probably earn yourself an express trip to Hell, if you haven't already."

The vehicle went around a curve, throwing Andrew against the side of the box.

"Hey! Watch it!"

More laughter. This guy was a regular chucklebutt. "A few bruises ain't gonna matter in a few minutes."

Andrew finally heard the ignition cut off, and a door opened. Someone pulled out the box and removed the lid.

"What the fuck is going on?" Andrew managed to sit up by holding on to the sides of the box, and looked around. He was in a warehouse full of blanket-covered boxes.

Except they weren't ordinary boxes. The casket sitting nearby proved it.

"Jesus Fucking Christ! I'm going to die!"

"That's right."

Fiona walked into view, and Andrew was struck by how gorgeous she was. Even here, about to die, he wanted to jump out of the box and bend her over the casket.

"Baby! Help!"

She shook her head. "You dumbass. I know everything." A man came into view, a bigger man in an oxford shirt and dress slacks. "You remember my cousin Lewis, right?"

Lewis. Lewis. Fuck, that name rang a bell.

"The undertaker," Lewis said with a helpful smile, and Andrew knew who had been driving the van.

"You sick son of a bitch!"

Fiona stepped forward and slapped him. "You're one to talk, all the time you spent down on Dixie Avenue. Am I not enough for you?"

"I thought you were at work. I was lonely!"

"Stupid fucker," Lewis muttered.

"Who asked you?" Andrew yelled.

Fiona slapped him again. "I could have lived with the whores, Andrew. If it was just them, you'd be crying on your mother's couch right now."

She walked over to the casket and picked up a manila folder lying on top. Watching her ass, Andrew felt himself getting hard.

A rubber mallet swung into view, smashing into his groin and shooting pain through his body. Andrew bent forward, a scream ripping through the building as the mortician laughed.

"Boy, you're a horn dog through and through. You're going to hell with a hard-on!"

Fiona shook her head, waiting for Andrew to recover. When he was able to sit up, she opened the folder and tossed it in his lap.

When he saw the screenshot, his heart sank.

Damn girl, you're so sexy. I know you said you have a boyfriend, but I wish you'd reconsider. There's so much I can do with this that he never could.

Underneath was a picture of his erect cock.

"Want to see the others? I stopped counting after eleven, but there's a line of angry women, boyfriends, and husbands who would love to get their hands on you." She leaned over to whisper in his ear. "Thanks to Lewis, they're all going to get a piece of you."

Andrew turned to look at the grinning mortician. "They're gonna defile your ass in ways you can't even imagine, buddy."

"You're going to cut me up?"

Lewis laughed. "God, no. That'd make too much of a mess." Grabbing the table the box was mounted on, he wheeled it over to a massive metal structure. Pushing a button, a door began to open.

"I'm also a crematory operator. This is my retort." Lewis grinned. "Actually, it's a lot of people's retort to your behavior…"

"Oh fuck! Please! No!" Andrew twisted, trying to look at Fiona. "You know I'm scared of fire!"

"Are you?" She looked down at her nails. "I guess if you'd thought about what other people wanted, I might be more inclined to think about what *you* want."

Lewis laughed, putting a cardboard roll in a groove at the front of the chamber. Stepping behind Andrew, he gave the box a shove, and it rolled inside.

"Any last words, you might want to get them out now," Lewis said. "This damn thing's walls are so thick, ain't no one gonna hear you scream. Especially not once the fire gets started."

"Fiona! Please!" Andrew yelled.

She bent over and kissed his forehead. "Goodbye, Andrew." He heard the motor as the door descended.

"Wait! No!"

The folder landed on top of him, screenshots floating around him like confetti.

Andrew smelled gas, then a clicking like a pilot light being lit. Flame erupted from the walls, consuming the cardboard and creeping toward him.

His scream was consumed by the retort.

ABOUT D.L. WINCHESTER

D.L. Winchester lives in the foothills of southern Appalachia. A former mortician, his work searches the darkness to find tales worth telling. He is the author of over three hundred obituaries, numerous short stories, and the upcoming flash fiction collection "A Terrible Place." In his spare time, he can be found searching for inspiration in the world around him and trying to keep his children from becoming the next generation of horror villains.

Liked this collection of stories? Check out D.L. Winchester's Shadows of Appalachia.

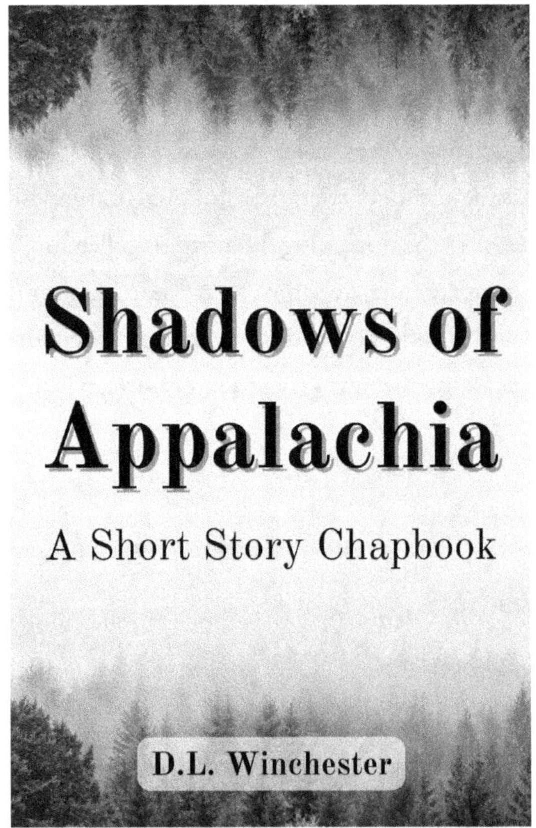

If you are a fan of horror stories and tales,
you'll want to follow Undertaker Books.

We're bringing you stories to take to your grave.
SIGN UP FOR OUR NEWSLETTER ONLINE

9 798990 617711